Cloudy, low 50s.
Showers tonight
and tomorrow.
Details page 125

Vol. 57. No. 50

DAILY

New York, Sun

שלום

Israel Gives Sadat a Rousing 'Shalom'

Prime Minister Menahem Begin welcomes President Anwar Sadat of Egypt in Israel yesterday.
Picture story in centerfold

Arab Brings 'Peace' Plan; Has 1st Talk With Begin

BRESLIN

On the Trail Of Sadat... And History

Four Pages of Coverage
Start on Page 2

The
Cairo Connection

Zola Levitt

Harvest House Publishers
Irvine, California 92714

THE CAIRO CONNECTION

Copyright © 1978 Harvest House Publishers
Irvine, California 92714
Library of Congress Catalog Card Number 77-94046
ISBN # 0-89081-127-X

Printed in the United States of America

CONTENTS

1

A Strange Marriage

Until November 20, 1977 A.D., Pharaoh had not come to Jerusalem in 4,000 years! Or at least when he did occasionally drop by, he would generally bring 100,000 troops.

But with the November, 1977 visit of President Anwar Sadat, Egypt's latter-day Pharaoh, the endless hostility was apparently broken. Peace was proposed by the Monarch of Egypt! And, if the proposal is accepted, a strange marriage will result. Who, in the long corridors of all that history . . . who, in the citadels of modern government . . . who, in his right mind, for that matter . . . would ever have expected any sort of alliance between Egypt and Israel?

If this is love, the whole world's crazy!

A DANGEROUS BOOK

Books written immediately after complicated political events can be very dangerous. Obviously, current "history" is extremely hard to estimate. The reader is forewarned that this is one of those dangerous books.

And yet, writing about current political events which have already been "covered" in the Bible is not nearly so hazardous. There is certainly no better book on the Israel-Egypt relationship than the Good Book, and fortunately the prophets gave a lot of space to these two important nations. Plenty of war and plenty of peace was foreseen by the prophets of the Old and New Testaments long before anything like the present day developments could even be suspected.

All in all, it should be realized that what is set down here in this brief space is an immediate reaction—a knee-jerk response—to what may well become one of the most profound international situations of the twentieth century. With the help of the Biblical analyses and the writings of certain scholars of prophecy, the author intends to show that peace between Israel and Egypt at this time is really not such a surprise after all. Despite the long history of animosity between these bad neighbors, a permanent peace is to be the net result of their relationship.

We are not seeing this permanent peace as yet, and it is probably a long way off. As a matter of fact, there is to be at least one other war—the fearful Armageddon—and the return of the Prince of Peace, according to the Scriptures, before anything like peaceful relations becomes a permanent reality between Israel and Egypt.

Read this book with caution, therefore, and expect many further developments in the Middle East as peace negotiations, complex ministrations behind the scenes, and the typical political double-crosses, progress. Use this book as a guide through the Biblical prophets, who spoke on the ultimate futures of Israel and Egypt. Use it as a thumbnail sketch, as it were, of the present situation. But don't use it as a perfectly reliable indicator of future events.

For a perfectly reliable indicator of future events, use the Bible.

WHY THIS BOOK?

There are many reasons for writing a book of this kind at this time. First of all, it is absolutely necessary to shed all possible light on Middle Eastern developments today. Unquestionably, the peace settlement intentions in this area of the world affect us all—every nation in every corner of the world. The Middle East has now become, as prophecy said it would be, the crossroads of the world and the central issue of the end times. But it is simply amazing how little attention has been given to the Biblical view of particularly Egypt in the latter days. This 5,000-year-old nation will certainly figure greatly in upcoming events. We "Johnnie-Come-Lately's" on the crazy quilt of shifting alliances between nations—the 200-year-old U.S.A., the 60-year-old U.S.S.R.—fail to appreciate the vitality and longevity of those ancient nations in the prime arena of God's activity.

The idea of peace between Israel and Egypt at this time could just possibly be a prophetic development of the utmost import. It may help to bring on the Russian invasion of Israel, which we will detail in Chapter 4. It may lead down the road to Armageddon, or, on the contrary, it may subvert and quiet the tensions which have been taking us toward those momentous events. In this book we will sketch the prophecies accurately which detail the end times events, and we will inform some readers of at least the general trends and directions. Naturally, there are always some people who do not know or respect prophecy at all, and they are invariably surprised by any new political development.

However, if Isaiah came walking down the street today, he could say, ''I told you so.''

Endless prophecy books have been written about the future of the believers and about the future of Israel. Very little has been said or written about the fascinating, upcoming career of Egypt, the Nation of the Pharaohs.

There are a great many churchgoing people— people who value the Bible and believe in an active and involved God—who still do not regard prophecy as important. The non-Bible reading world might well be expected to think of the prophetic portions of the Bible as so many fables, but it is downright disheartening to find that there are some *believers* in this category. As developments continue inexorably to follow the pre-announced plan of God for this world, more and more people of both camps are beginning to appreciate the accuracy and validity of God's Word, but there will always be those to whom the Christian faith is a here-and-now affair with nothing of importance to be said about the future. What we see is what we get, they feel. If this book can help in some small way to alter that view, its prime purpose will be realized.

Secondly, this is a book about salvation, with a serious, evangelical purpose. It will not depart from the technical realities of prophetic Scripture to preach sermons or make invitations, but it has, as its foundation, the soundness of the belief in the God of creation and of the redemption provided to all by His Son, Jesus Christ. In Israel, at the time of the coming of God's Son, there were those familiar with prophetic Scripture about the Messiah and those who were not. Some could recognize the Carpenter of Galilee as the fulfillment of Isaiah 53, or Daniel 9:25, or Psalm 22, or Genesis 3:15, or Isaiah 9:6-7. They lined the road to the Temple site in such numbers that the opposing Pharisees could be heard to exclaim, "Behold, the world is gone after Him," (John 12:19). The ones unfamiliar with, or disrespectful of, prophecy concerning this event—the very coming of the Messiah—remained in unrelieved unbelief.

The knowledge of prophecy in that case made the difference of life and death, and we are in a like situation again today. The King is coming again and those who are aware of the prophecies about this event will be the ones ready for His arrival. The ones unaware of the prophecies will line up again with those who watched fulfillment after fulfillment in the gospel and still saw nothing. Peace covenants will come and go, invasions and a great war will come and go, but the Prince of Peace will come and stay to establish His Kingdom on earth for those who believe in Him.

May this short study of what may be a deeply significant, prophetic event turn the non-watchers of prophecy into people who grow excited at the ongoing plan of Almighty God, and who are thus moved to seek salvation through the atoning ministry of His Son.

WILBUR MOOREHEAD SMITH (B. 1894)

A little cursory research in a public library will show that the most thorough—indeed, perhaps the only—book on Egypt in prophecy is a work by the respected theologian, Wilbur Moorehead Smith. Apart from stray remarks in Bible commentaries and perhaps a theological treatise here and there, there seems to be no other thorough study of this important matter extant today.

Professor Smith became excited by the War of 1956, another of the Egyptian exercises which failed to invade Israel. The definitive book *Egypt in Biblical Prophecy*, published by W. A. Wilde Company, Boston, Massachusetts, 1957, was the result. This author is deeply indebted to the painstaking and very complete research of Wilbur Smith for many of the observations on prophecy in this present book.

Smith, a very experienced theological researcher, set out to study the whole subject of Egypt in Israel's history and assumed he would find a wealth of material at any library. He admits in his author's preface that if he had taken an examination covering Egypt in Biblical prophecy, he would have flunked it, since he had not given the subject any attention prior to the War of 1956. But he was stunned to find that even at the New York Public Library, where two massive bibliographies of material on ancient Egypt, covering 16,000 items, were listed, there was not a single reference to the Biblical prophecies about Egypt! Try as he would, Dr. Smith was unable to uncover even the most cursory study of this more and more urgent issue of prophecy. Thus, Smith felt obliged to dig deeply into the Scriptures and to prepare a full length book containing a detailed analysis of prophecy (a whole chapter on Isaiah 19 alone, which begins with the phrase, ''The Burden of Egypt''); and the subject, at least up through 1956, was at last adequately covered.

Naturally, we must now go on from there.

Smith, in all his patient research and with the help of the writings of Isaiah, Ezekiel, Jeremiah, Daniel, et. al., was able to accurately deal with Egypt in the Tribulation period and the Kingdom. But, of course, he was not able to foresee the world-shaking consequences of the 1967 War, which regained the Old City of Jerusalem and the Temple site for Israel, nor the 1973 War, which brought the menace of Russia and her enormous power to the Middle East. Now, with the new peace offer from Sadat, the scene has changed still again. We might say, in all candor, that if some author had started out in 1948, the date of the recovery of the Promised Land by the Jewish people, to chronicle the events leading straight up to the Tribulation period and the return of the Lord, he would have been kept steadily busy, almost like a newspaper reporter.

It is a fact that Smith's book is probably too complex for most lay readers. This author, a sometime student of prophecy and steady reader of the Bible, was overwhelmed by the profundities to be found in those massive sections of the Old Testament so often neglected in so many churches. The expositions and conclusions of Smith require a most qualified reader of theology to appreciate, and that brings forth another reason for this particular book. Hopefully, in the pages that follow, there will be a clear and simplified understanding of the prophetic trends associated with the latest Israel-Egypt developments that will be well within the comprehension of the lay reader, and still treat the subject profitably.

And hopefully more books will come forth chronicling the ever more intense and ever more obvious progression of events leading to the conclusion of God's plan for the world as we know it. It remains a great enigma that the vast majority of the citizens of the world—even those of the Middle East, and those of the Biblical churches— are still mystified by the ongoing development of what has already been detailed in the Word of God. More books, and better books, will hopefully be available to correct this situation as time goes on.

Some people have always studied prophecy and have obtained great rewards, but it is safe to say that the present generation has more reason to understand prophecy than any before it.

THE ROAD TO ARMAGEDDON

It may seem a bit dramatic to say that the current Middle Eastern events are an expected stopover along the road to Armageddon, but actually there is much justification for that. The ensuing chapters of this book will attempt to connect this latest attempt at a peace covenant with the ultimate war to end this age.

In the next chapter, we will consider the impact of the modern Pharaoh's trip to Jerusalem, as well as the past relations between Egypt and Israel. Again, when we say "past relations," we are talking about a *very* long past. Pharaoh has met some challenging Israeli personalities before, such as Abraham, Joseph, Moses and the like. The rulers of Egypt, from the ancient Pharaohs to the modern Moslems (who are not really historically connected, if the truth be told), have ever maintained very shaky relations with the Chosen People. We will show that the Sadat peace proposal is truly a one-of-a-kind event, something that virtually never happened before in recorded history.

In the third chapter, we will consider the segments of opposition to Sadat's peace move, which are formidable. To say that the PLO and the other Arab nations are annoyed is to greatly understate the situation. To assert that the Russians are astonished and infuriated comes somewhat closer. To state that the Americans are merely delighted is to perhaps show our indifference and ignorance where the prophetic picture is concerned. It is a certainty that the whole world is watching, and that Anwar Sadat is not among its most popular national administrators at the moment.

In the fourth chapter, we can confidently announce, with Ezekiel, that "the Russians are coming." The new peace offer by Sadat is, in its way, one of the most important and interesting dominoes in the whole "domino theory" of Communist expansion. Sadat's overtures for peace may not come out as peaceful as he thinks. People who know prophecy are seeing Red.

The section to follow, on the Antichrist, is not so fanciful as it might seem. The constant attempts of those who wish to identify the Antichrist before he chooses to come forward have been greatly gratified by Sadat's latest move. Almost anyone in public life can be suspected to be the Antichrist these days, as we shall see, but Sadat's curious identification with that "man of peace" conception of the Antichrist has tempted some prophecy analysts. We shall consider, in that chapter, if it is at all reasonable to suppose that this latest Middle Eastern development in any way heralds the entrance of this fearsome figure.

And finally the book will conclude with the Biblical picture of the Kingdom to come, when it can be said in all certainty that Israel and Egypt will remain at peace permanently. Following along that road to Armageddon, we must pass many dangerous corners, but in the end God will surely prevail, and there will be "Peace on earth, good will toward men."

So let us now begin with the visit of Sadat and Premier Begin and the interesting four-millennia background to the present situation.

2

Pharaoh Comes to Jerusalem

To appreciate the magnitude of the Sadat trip, we should consider it against the background of Israel-Egypt relations. It's a long and stormy story of rivalry, jealousy, bullying, as well as an ongoing clash of religious faiths. It might be safe to say that nowhere in the world, for such a long period of time, has there ever existed more uncomfortable neighbors.

Egypt, to give it its due, is one of the most important geographical and cultural areas of world history. Asia and Africa meet in Egypt, and there once arose in that land the most advanced and cultured civilization of the ancient world. It is well to remember that the Egyptians were building the massive pyramids—monuments to engineering, patience and egotism—some 2,000 years before the flowering of ancient Greece. Egyptian science, medicine, government and agriculture were the envy of a world so ancient that the majority of its human members were what we think of as "prehistoric."

With all of that, the ancient Egyptians were a warring people, and those who lived close by, as did the Israelis, suffered through endless contentions.

ABRAHAM AND PHARAOH

The very first instance of relations between Israel and Egypt concerns the rather unmeritorious behavior of the father of the Chosen People toward the ruler of the Nile.

The Canaanite Abraham felt compelled to go down into Egypt to avoid famine in the Promised Land, and there, for fear of the Egyptians (to hear him tell it) he introduced his wife as his sister. The beautiful and exotic Sarah, Mesopotamian by birth, would tempt the Egyptians, Abraham felt, and they might kill him in their covetousness. King David, 1,000 years later, would not be above such lusty behavior, and Abraham felt it would be best to be alive as the brother of the bride.

Unfortunately, no less a personage than Pharaoh became enamored with Sarah and Abraham was delighted to receive gifts from the well-to-do suitor in exchange for his good will. But God was not pleased, understandably, and the palace of Pharaoh was smitten with Divine judgment. The remarkable story, told in Genesis 12:10-20, concludes with the pagan king ordering out of Egypt as morally unfit, the friend of God!

The first *prophecy* that mentions Egypt in the Bible is still of fundamental importance today and seems almost designed to cause trouble in the Middle East, from our perspective. God chose to establish generous boundaries for the nation of Israel:

> "In the same day the Lord made a cove-
> nant with Abram, saying, Unto thy seed
> have I given this land, from the river of
> Egypt unto the great river, the river
> Euphrates" (Gen. 15:18).

While Israel did occupy very nearly that much territory in the great days of David and Solomon a millennium later on, many today apply this prophecy to coming times and consider that Israel's expansion into the presently explosive, occupied territories is only a logical step toward the ultimate fulfillment. Egypt probably did not like the prophecy when it was uttered, and likes it still less today.

In the same Biblical chapter, the Almighty pronounced less happy news for Israel in prophesying what was to become the real bone of contention in the Middle East:

> "And he said unto Abram, 'Know of a surety that thy seed shall be a stranger in a land that is not their's, and shall serve them; and they shall afflict them four hundred years;
>
> And also that nation, whom they shall serve, will I judge: and afterward shall they come out with great substance,' " (Gen. 15:13-14).

Israel indeed went into slavery to Egypt for some four centuries, emerging finally in the magnificent Exodus.

PHARAOH, THE HARDHEARTED

Before that unhappy experience, however, Abraham's great grandson, Joseph, rose to magnificent heights in the Egyptian government. Called in Scripture "Lord of all Egypt" (Gen. 45:9), Joseph, through his skillful interpretations of Pharaoh's dreams and his administrative acumen, had become the Vice Pharaoh of the mighty nation. It's just possible that since the happy days of Pharaoh and his valued assistant, the Israelite Joseph, Israeli-Egyptian relations were never so good until Sadat and Begin.

Joseph, in truth, had done great favors for Egypt through the power of God, who had revealed to him an upcoming seven years of famine. The Vice Pharaoh planned ahead accordingly, and spared the land of the Nile a season of poverty that affected virtually the entire Middle East.

But other Pharaohs came and went, and the Israelites, still sojourners in a strange land, became just another minority group. Forgotten was the brilliance of the gifted Joseph as the later rulers enslaved the Chosen People. God was moved. He later told Moses:

> "I have surely seen the affliction of my people which are in Egypt, and have heard their cry by reason of their task-masters; for I know their sorrows," (Exodus 3:7).

The idea of four centuries of slavery is simply incomprehensible in the world today. No people now living have suffered so much for so long. The

Israelites toiled under the lash to build the mighty Egyptian monuments and, on the occasion when their champion Moses came before the infinitely hardhearted Pharaoh of the Exodus, suffered the ignominy of having their work purposely made even harder.

The Exodus, of course, is a historical and spiritual event of unequaled magnitude. Worldly freedom, spiritual salvation and a new standard of liberty on the national level is established for all time in this dramatic deliverance.

Surely the Jews of today do not hold the present occupiers of the territory of Egypt responsible for the centuries of slavery, but it should be appreciated that for a long time after the Exodus the Old Testament rings with the phrase, "We were Pharaoh's bondmen." Some have likened the ten plagues, by which God finally judged and punished Egypt at the time of the Exodus, to Egypt's poor condition today. A case can certainly be made out of the Bible for God's reacting to various peoples in accordance with how they treat the Jews:

> "And I will bless them that bless thee, and curse him that curseth thee: and in thee shall all families of the earth be blessed," (Gen. 12:3).

"And the King shall answer and say unto
them, Verily I say unto you, Inasmuch as
ye have done it unto one of the least of
these my brethren, ye have done it unto
me," (Matt. 25:40).

Some feel that Egypt's continuing animosity
since 1948 (no less than four attempted invasions),
has earned her the poverty and various other
troubles visited upon her now.

SOLOMON IN ALL HIS GLORY

The Bible is silent about Egypt between the
Exodus and the reign of Solomon, a period of
some four more centuries. That singular sovereign,
in all his glory, "made affinity with Pharaoh, King
of Egypt, and took Pharaoh's daughter, and
brought her into the city of David . . ." (I Kings
3:1). This cannot be called a special gesture of
Israeli friendship toward Egypt, however, since
Solomon quite regularly and successfully made
alliances with the neighboring kings. And he was
without peer at bringing their daughters home to
Jerusalem, having collected 700 wives and 300
concubines.

Nonetheless, Solomon maintained lively trade
with his neighbor to the south:

"And Solomon had horses brought out of Egypt, and linen yarn: the king's merchants received the linen yarn at a price.

And a chariot came up and went out of Egypt for six hundred shekels of silver, and an horse for an hundred and fifty: and so for all the kings of the Hitites, and for the kings of Syria, did they bring them out by their means," (I Kings 10:28-29).

Relations between the two nations seemed neighborly enough at that time, though Solomon, who "ruled over all the kings from the river (the Euphrates) even unto the land of the Philistines, and to the border of Egypt," (II Chron. 9:26), must have been a good friend to have. At least on the mercantile level, Egypt conducted amicable enough relations with the now mighty nation-state of Israel.

A NATION DIVIDED

But the good neighbor policy didn't last. After the death of Solomon, Israel became divided into northern and southern kingdoms, and the

Egyptian King Shisshak marched on Judah and Israel (I Kings 14:25-28). Shisshak plundered the very House of God:

> "And he took away the treasures of the house of the Lord, and the treasures of the king's house; he even took away all: and he took away all the shields of gold which Solomon had made," (I Kings 14:26).

The weak southern kingdom of Judah staggered on, enduring invasions from all sides through the times of the Kings. Egypt arrived regularly with soldiers and chariots, accomplishing particularly disastrous results under Pharaoh-nechoh.

Nechoh was an imperialist, bent on the expansion of Egypt into Asia Minor. He sailed a mighty armada on the Mediterranean and the Red Sea, and invaded the land of the Philistines. Pushing northward, he encountered the young King Josiah (c. 650-610 B.C.) in the Valley of Megiddo. Josiah, King of Judah, hopelessly outnumbered and outgunned, tried to resist the terrible force of Egypt.

Even God seemed to mourn the death of the reverent Josiah:

"And like unto him was there no king
before him, that turned to the Lord with
all his heart, and with all his soul, and
with all his might, according to all the
law of Moses; neither after him arose
there any like him," (II Kings 23:25).

The ambitious Nechoh exacted a heavy tribute
from Israel:

"And Pharaoh-nechoh made Eliakim,
the son of Josiah, king in the room of
Josiah his father, and turned his name to
Jehoiakim, and took Jehoahaz away: and
he came to Egypt, and died there.

And Jehoiakim gave the silver and the
gold to Pharaoh; but he taxed the land
to give the money according to the com-
mandment of Pharaoh: he exacted the
silver and the gold of the people of the
land, of every one according to his taxa-
tion, to give it unto Pharaoh-nechoh,"
(II Kings 23:34-35).

It seems that Nechoh's fondest dreams of
Egyptian expansion would have been realized had
it not been for the immensely powerful Nebuchad-

nezzar of Babylon. This nearly invincible conqueror, at the head of a gigantic and well-drilled army, repelled the Egyptians, invaded Judah, wrecked Solomon's Temple and conquered far and wide—creating a Middle Eastern empire that only Alexander the Great was able to overcome, some two centuries later.

Some of the population of Judah had fled into Egypt, to avoid the advance of Nebuchadnezzar from the north. And, with that remnant, God was particularly infuriated. Through Jeremiah the Prophet, He decreed a terrible doom for all those who had resorted to pagan Egypt, from which, after all, the Almighty had chosen to withdraw His people earlier:

> "Therefore thus saith the Lord of hosts, the God of Israel; Behold, I will set my face against you for evil, and to cut off all Judah.

> And I will take the remnant of Judah, that have set their faces to go into the land of Egypt to sojourn there, and they shall all be consumed, and fall in the land of Egypt; they shall even be consumed by the sword and by the famine: they shall die, from the least even unto the greatest, by the sword and by the

famine: and they shall be an execration, and an astonishment, and a curse, and a reproach.

For I will punish them that dwell in the land of Egypt, as I have punished Jerusalem, by the sword, by the famine, and by the pestilence:

So that none of the remnant of Judah, which are gone into the land of Egypt to sojourn there, shall escape or remain, that they should return into the land of Judah, to the which they have a desire to return to dwell there: for none shall return but such as shall escape," (Jeremiah 44:11-14).

That God Himself had some distaste for Egypt, it may not be fair to say, but it is most apparent that He hated the idea of His Chosen People living in that land, even to avoid captivity by Babylon. In point of fact, we hear no more of that remnant which fled to Egypt and presumably the Almighty dealt with them exactly in accordance with His curse. Perhaps the only Jews who ever survived that retreat into Egypt were "such as shall escape."

The Old Testament record closes without

further important mention of Egypt, and, in fact, for the rest of the B.C. centuries, both Israel and Egypt became mere provinces of foreign powers. Alexander, and then Rome, occupied both lands, and neither had autonomy enough to give the other much trouble.

Thus throughout the two millennia preceding the coming of Christ, the relations between Egypt and Israel can be described as fitfully alternating between occasional trade and all-out war. Nothing like true peace seems implied either in the Scriptures or secular history; although alliances of mutual profit and convenience did occur.

JESUS TO BEGIN

The most fascinating mention of Egypt in the gospels concerns the retreat there of the Lord Himself. His parents were obliged to flee the tyranny of Herod, who was determined to kill all of the male infants of Bethlehem in his effort to thwart the coming of the prophesied King of the Jews. This short sojourn in Egypt of the infant Jesus seemed a subtle part of God's overall plan for His Chosen People. Compare the New and Old Testament Scriptures:

> "And was there (in Egypt) until the death of Herod: that it might be fulfilled which was spoken of the Lord by the prophet, saying, Out of Egypt have I called my Son," (Matt. 2:15).

> "When Israel was a child, then I loved him, and called my son out of Egypt," (Hosea 11:1).

Thus a microcosm of the Exodus itself is relived in the career of the Messiah of the Jews.

MOHAMMED (B. 570 A.D.)

From the gospel times onward, Egypt and Israel were each to undergo extraordinary changes. The Jews were dispersed, of course, beginning with the sacking of the Second Temple of God by Titus of Rome in 70 A.D. The dispersion was all but completed and Israel entirely taken out of Jewish hands by the anti-Semite Hadrian, the Roman Emperor who chose to build the Temple of Jupiter on the original Temple site in Jerusalem in 135 A.D. The Jews thus became the nomads of the world, not to return to their Promised Land in any great numbers until 1948!

For their part, the Egyptians were to undergo an

entire change of character and religion. The country had become thoroughly Hellenized and boasted of a magnificent library in Alexandria which contained the great writings of the Greeks. They were thoroughly Romanized as well; a taxpaying tributary of that mightiest of the ancient empires. But, as Rome declined and Christianity flourished, Egypt was somewhat off the beaten path of the emerging Western civilization. And with the birth of the Arabian, Mohammed, in 570 A.D., the Egyptian civilization was to undergo its most basic change in all of its history.

The amazing conquest and conversion of the entire Mediterranean world by the Islam faith is one of the remarkable triumphs of modern paganism. Egypt was overrun by nomadic Arabs, who first attacked and then converted virtually the entire nation. The magnificent library of Alexandria was looted and destroyed, but it was considered no great loss by the believers of the Koran. They already had all wisdom, they felt, and indeed they galvanized all of their immense territory into a frantic but highly unified spiritual force.

Though the dispersed Jews and the Moslem Egyptians had little contact in these times, the Islam religion made a move that is of the utmost import today. Choosing Jerusalem as the third most holy city of the Islam faith (since the prophet Mohammed had visited there and, they believed, stepped off from the very Temple site when he rode his horse to heaven), they constructed the Dome of the Rock on the ruins of the Temple of Jupiter. This golden-domed, mosaic-tiled structure now stands in the center of Israeli occupied Jerusalem, on the ancient Temple site, forcing Jew and Arab to live together at least on a thirty-four acre religious site.

The Dome of the Rock is one great bone of contention in today's Middle Eastern power struggle. According to prophecy, its days are numbered, since it stands on the very site of the future Tribulation Temple (see *Satan in the Sanctuary*, Moody Press, 1973, by Dr. Thomas S. McCall and the author). This may be a very bad time to own "a piece of the Rock."

Amazingly, the very rock which still stands inside the Dome is illustrative of Israeli-Egyptian differences. Today's Egyptians, Moslem to the core, hold that Mohammed's horse indeed stepped off from this very rock. The Jewish tradition is that it was on this rock Abraham offered Isaac, "thine only son," in sacrifice to the God of Israel. (President Sadat made his pilgrimage to the Temple site during his visit to Israel, kneeling in prayer at the nearby Al Aksa Mosque, the male equivalent of the Dome of the Rock which is reserved for women's prayer.)

THE WANDERING JEWS

Apart from the Dome of the Rock standing on its rather sensitive acreage, the nations of Israel and Egypt hardly encountered each other throughout the entire A.D. years. Jews were to be found throughout the world and even in Egypt, of course, but new contention did not really arise until the start of Zionism in the 19th century, and the slow but steady return of Jews to Israel. Egypt stood by, nervously watching its ancient neighbors slipping back into the land throughout the first half of the 20th century.

In 1948, however, the Egyptians bore arms. With the United Nations' decision to partition the land of Israel and readmit the Jews of the world, the attitude of the hardhearted Pharaohs seemed reborn.

And, of course, within most every reader's memory now is the vicious succession of four real wars—in 1948, 1956, 1967 and 1973—in which the two ancient foes met again on the fields of bloody battle. There has almost been a regular schedule of military conflict since the independence of Israel in 1948, and the relationship has been of such animosity that it has been very difficult for many people to believe that Sadat really wants peace.

Against that backdrop, then, let us now take a close look at the visit of President Anwar Sadat.

In view of all that's happened between these two nations, can we now reasonably expect anything like a just and lasting peace?

THE SADAT TRIP

"It could not have been more improbable or unexpected. It was as if a messenger from Allah had descended to the Promised Land on a magic carpet," rhapsodized *Time* magazine (November 28, 1977).

New York Governor Carey called the Sadat visit, "The greatest exercise in my memory in bringing peace to the entire world," (New York Times, November 22, 1977).

Prime Minister Begin followed suit:

> "During the visit, a momentous agreement was achieved already—no more

war, no more bloodshed, no more attacks and collaboration to avoid any event which may lead to such tragic developments . . . It is a great moral achievement for our nation, for the Middle East, indeed, for the whole world,'' (New York Times, November 22, 1977).

President Sadat instructed the people of Israel to "teach your children that what has passed is the end of suffering, and what will come is a new life," (*Time*, November 28, 1977).

One of Sadat's aides, upon seeing the brilliant red carpet laid out at Tel Aviv's Ben Gurion Airport and the huge sign, WELCOME TO ISRAEL, PRESIDENT SADAT, in Arabic, Hebrew and English, just about summed up the sentiments of the whole world:

"Just look at that. I never would have believed it!" (*Time*, November 28, 1977).

The Sunday, November 20, 1977 edition of The New York Daily News came out with a gigantic headline in Hebrew—"SHALOM!", and a picture of a beaming Begin and a satisfied, personable Sadat on the front page.

The New Yorker magazine paid Sadat a magnificent tribute:

> "As with his speech, the strength did not depend on outward things, but came from inside Sadat himself. Nothing could change that. The manifest sincerity of his conviction and the action that followed upon it were real, not symbolic, and throughout the trip that reality came through steady and strong. The onlookers vacillated between hope and despair, idealism and cynicism, but always there was Sadat: unruffled, thoughtfully attentive, not posturing in any way, never striking a false note—just a man, a very fine man, who had made a decision because he thought it right, and, without illusions, was carrying it out. It was not an act, it was a deed, and, whatever happened, the integrity of that deed stood. Whatever happens in the future, it will still stand." (Dec. 5, 1977)

The reportage could, of course, go on and on. Every newspaper and magazine virtually the world around remarked on the unprecedented event. We will not belabor the details here; it was in all ways a very typical diplomatic trip, except, of course, in the characters involved and the fact that their two countries were still virtually at war. It seemed to be a two-day exercise of ever so cautious approaches to problems of real magnitude; and it had its expected press conferences, overblown reportage, lofty closing statements and all the rest of the peculiar trappings of the high affairs of state.

Probably no reader of this book is uninformed about what happened in Jerusalem and the subsequent developments. The Geneva Conference, seemingly perpetually in the planning stage, will apparently be the real workshop for the many issues advanced, clarified, agreed upon and disagreed upon in Jerusalem. Preliminary meetings leading to Geneva are expected to drag out for some time, at this writing.

And then beyond the Geneva Conference, there comes, if we read prophecy accurately, the Russian invasion of Israel, the Antichrist, Armageddon, the second coming of the Lord and the Kingdom on earth. This is not to make the Geneva Conference seem unimportant, but to stress that in a story of a search for peace that has taken so many thousands of years, no one event, save the return of the Prince of Peace, can be much more than the briefest of stopovers.

GOLDA'S WARNING

The author had a peculiar experience in connection with this entire series of Middle Eastern events because of what transpired in Dallas, Texas, just a week before. The General Assembly of the Jewish Council of Federations, an umbrella group encompassing the work of several American Jewish organizations committed to the support of Israel and American Jewry, held a conference in Dallas, November 10-12. The author was invited to attend as a news correspondent.

Some very noteworthy speakers were involved— U.S. Secretary of State Cyrus Vance, Israeli Ambassador to the U.S. Simchah Dinitz, and former Prime Minister of Israel (and outspoken critic of Sadat) Golda Meir. Totally unaware, of course, that there was about to be some kind of "peace breakthrough" in the Middle East the very next week, the gathered 2,000 delegates heard some pre-Sadat-trip Israeli views.

Ambassador Dinitz warned about rising anti-Semitism everywhere in the world, including the United States. Secretary of State Vance continued to call for orderly negotiations toward peace in the Middle East, reading a prepared and cautiously worded speech. But Mrs. Meir was more emphatic and more eloquent. The headline in the Sunday, November 13, Dallas Morning News seemed a bit shocking:

"GOLDA MEIR WARNS JEWS ABOUT SADAT"

Considering that Mrs. Meir was photographed scarcely a week later in huge smiles with President Sadat (and they effusively congratulated each other on their various grandchildren, etc., etc.) her remarks at the earlier conference surely show the vagaries of modern international politics.

Morning News reporter Bill Kenyon began his article, "Former Israeli Prime Minister Golda Meir told an emotional group of Jewish leaders here Saturday that Egyptian President Anwar Sadat's recent public pleas for peace have a hollow ring because 'This is not a peace-loving man.' " Mrs. Meir went on to say, "Sadat makes a speech about peace and everyone says 'Bravo,' while Israel, year after year, has been ready to negotiate." She concluded her remarks with a statement she later repeated to Sadat in Jerusalem, "I hope to still be alive to bring the message, 'We've made it, peace in Israel.' ''

Significant in the Dallas conference was Ambassador Dinitz' emphasis on the fact that Israel had already issued a personal invitation to Sadat for the big visit. Most news sources afterward indicated that the peace visit was entirely Sadat's idea.

BROTHERLY LOVE?

Once the peace visit had taken place, the Morning News ran an article with quite a bit of contrast. Written again by reporter Kenyon, the headline read:

> "SADAT TRIP PEACE STEP, RABBI
> SAYS"

This time the commentator was Rabbi Max Zucker, President of the Dallas Rabbinical Association and Rabbi of the Dallas orthodox congregation. This article began significantly, "Egyptian President Anwar Sadat's recent visit to Israel not only signals the first steps toward peace in the Middle East, but is also a sign of the fulfillment of Biblical prophecy." Rabbi Zucker felt that Sadat's visit "is a repeat of Jacob and Esau. God has opened up the Bible to us once again."

Curiously, the portion of the Bible set aside for study at the week beginning sundown, Saturday, November 19 (the very moment of Sadat's arrival in Israel), was Genesis, chapters 32-36, the story of Jacob's return to meet his brother, Esau. "The events had to be on that specific date approved by the Divine Hand," analyzed Rabbi Zucker.

True enough, Jacob and Esau were able to reconcile their differences and their previously stormy relationship saw much better days after that historic meeting. But it is difficult to take seriously the Rabbi's delineation of this particular patriarchal event as prophecy. In the final three chapters of this book, we will review with the appropriate Scriptures the possible prophetic significance of the Sadat visit. In view of the wealth of genuine Biblical prophecy, identified as such in the Scriptures, we will be able to draw more exact parallels than the reconciliation of Jacob and Esau. Rabbi Zucker concluded his remarks on a most positive note: "Next year when I take my group to Israel, I hope they can stay in the Cairo Hilton."

CONFLICT IN CAIRO

At the time of this writing, it looks extremely doubtful that any rabbis will be staying at the Cairo Hilton during the coming year, despite all of the further talk in Cairo resulting from the original visit of President Sadat. Again, the mission of Sadat, apart from all of its drama (the *Time* cover called it ''Sadat's 'Sacred' Mission''), seemed to many commentators only the vaguest of opening bids in a very long game of war and peace.

In this brief section on the Sadat visit, we have considered mainly the positive reactions. But if one were to count heads in the Middle East—particularly heads of state—the negatives would far outweigh the positives. In the following chapter, we will try to assess the very formidable difficulties that lie ahead as the not-so-popular President Sadat now confronts his traditional Arab allies, the Russians, the United Nations, and those ever present tough customers, the chosen people of the Promised Land.

3

The Cairo Connection

At the time of this writing, the Cairo peace conference, such as it is, is in progress. Prime Minister Begin is in Washington, conferring with President Carter. The Arabs who are hostile to Sadat have just finished their bitter conversations in Tripoli, and the Soviets are sulking about all these new developments.

This could easily be the most inaccurate chapter of this book, since it is being written almost simultaneously with the events. Nevertheless, it is hoped some light might be shed on what will undoubtedly be a lengthy and tortuous progression of peace talks leading up to the Geneva Convention, if that really happens.

At the present time, the Cairo peace talks look like a big flop compared to the excitement of Jerusalem shortly before. The meetings were started at the lower echelon with neither Sadat nor Begin attending, as if in admission that the road ahead is tiring, steep and filled with pitfalls. The two statesmen who head their respective governments seemed exhausted from negotiating, smiling and otherwise posturing in the bright light of world acclaim in Jerusalem. They have withdrawn and sent in their specialty teams. And the peace drama, so promising in Jerusalem, looks at this point like it won't play in Cairo.

Sadat, for a moment the Lion of Judah, seems almost banished from the Arab world.

DOWN WITH SADAT

An Associated Press item of Tuesday, November 29, pointed out how few potential members of the Cairo Conference valued their invitations. The opening paragraph stated:

> "Israel formally agreed Monday to attend President Anwar Sadat's preliminary peace conference in Cairo. But no one else did, and the radical governments of Libya and Iraq separately called anti-Sadat Arab summits in their capitals."

To consider the various reactions of those receiving invitations to Cairo, we will go once around the Middle East to see how few chose to dance to Sadat's new tune.

First of all, in Israel, Prime Minister Begin immediately accepted the invitation and named two top aides as his envoys. At the same time, he rejected Sadat's implicit calls for Israeli withdrawal from all Arab territories occupied in 1967 and the establishment of a Palestinian state. To Begin, those, of course, run from matters that are negotiable at such conferences to concessions that are unthinkable.

Israel's true position is easy to understand, in view of the Middle Eastern scene since 1948. The return of certain occupied lands is considered within reason and indeed Begin was expected to propose the same to President Carter, at least as regards the Sinai. The Golan Heights, the demilitarized area between Israel and ever-crouching Syria, is much less of a negotiable territory, being regarded by the Israelis as a life-or-death buffer zone. The history of hostility from the Syrians, not to mention the constant troubles on the northern border since the time of Abraham and Lot, precludes the return of very much of the Golan territory.

As to the West Bank, Begin was expected to propose something like a joint Israeli-Arab administration of the territory, or self-rule by the local Palestinians, but certainly no out-and-out return of the area to Jordan. Again, the Israelis require a buffer zone, and Begin is fond of referring to the West Bank as "Judea and Samaria," in which he is Biblically precise. The establishment of a true Palestinian state is probably one of the unthinkable concessions, since the Israelis consider that that would be inviting disaster—to give the desecrators of Ma'alot and the olympic games neighboring land on which to drill their terrorists is simply out of the question in the Israeli mind.

And, finally, the return of Jerusalem would qualify as the most unthinkable of the unthinkables. Probably no one in the world seriously expects the Jews to give up their capital city, established in the time of King David and filled with Jewish relics of the ages. Before they would return any portion of Jerusalem, the Israelis would fight to the last man to defend it.

But, in any case, Begin responded amicably to his invitation to Cairo, sent proper representation and went off to Washington to confer with President Carter and a jumpy U.S. government.

Across the Jordan, King Hussein tried to walk on both sides of the street. He declared that he was ready to attend both the Tripoli and Cairo meetings, thus both supporting and denouncing Sadat, if we properly understand the atmospheres of those meetings. He pleaded with Arabs to "reunite ranks and rebuild a unified position."

Hussein, the ever hesitant Hamlet of the Arab world, heads one of the confrontation states but has little to confront anybody with. The weak Jordanian military bothered Israel very little in the previous conflicts and indeed Hussein usually loses much more than he gains in opposing his much stronger neighbor to the west.

The dependably hostile Syrian President Hafez Assad took his usual pose of hatred toward Israel and was up to his normal mischief concerning any peace with that nation. He chose to accept the invitation to Tripoli "to discuss ways and means to foil the results of Sadat's Israeli trip." He was even willing to end his feud with Iraq to spite Sadat and to maintain a united front against the Egyptian president. Assad's occasional claims that he wants peace in the Middle East cannot be taken seriously; he has never shown the vaguest initiative in that direction, but seems to prefer smashing and smashing again against the northern border of the Promised Land in the hopes of ever more gravely wounding his mortal enemy.

Iraq decided to hold its own summit conference, inviting Algeria, Libya, South Yemen, Syria and all of the Palestinian guerilla groups. Iraq can be counted on for friendly relations with Israel only after the King comes and establishes peace on earth.

Syria sent its foreign minister to Moscow, and Iraq said it would also send a spokesman there.

The United States agreed to attend the Cairo Conference in an observational role, along with representatives of the United Nations.

For its part, the Palestine Liberation Organization (PLO) accused Sadat of trying to bargain away Palestinian rights. Speaking at the United Nations, Faruk Kaddumi, PLO Political Department head, told the General Assembly that Sadat's visit to Israel was "a departure from the course that might lead to the Geneva Peace Conference." The PLO will achieve peaceful relations with Israel only after they have killed out the Israelis to the last man, it would appear.

Lebanon, still reeling from its lengthy civil war and trying to maintain its precarious neutrality in the Arab-Israeli conflict, declined to attend either conference.

To summarize the situation, no one was really very interested in Cairo except Israel and Egypt.

Virtually all of the Arab states, to greater or lesser degrees, condemned President Sadat, and were overwhelmingly against the idea of even talking about peace with Israel.

The whole demonstration goes to show that the only ones who want peace between Egypt and Israel are Egypt and Israel.

PHARAOH LIVES

As much as Egypt is presently praising its leader for his peace initiative, rivalry and hatred toward Israel has been a fact of life in that nation for a long, long time. The Koran itself, the holy book of largely Moslem Egypt, subtly defames the Jews and insists that they be conquered. While Sadat's attitude seems to be a politically advisable course presently, and while the population at large seems to approve, a change in the heart of every Egyptian may be a long time in coming.

The author's book about the Yom Kippur War, *Israel in Agony*, (Harvest House, 1975) chronicled an Egyptian attitude of anti-Semitism that would have gratified the Red Sea Pharaoh. Particularly illuminating in the author's research for this former book was a little shirt-pocket booklet carried into battle by all Egyptian soldiers. It was obtained at the Israel Army Information Center in Tel Aviv and it contained the original Arabic text with facing pages translated into English. The booklet clearly demonstrated the Islamic position on Israel and how this philosophy inspires the Egyptian soldier to a fierce hatred of the Jews.

The introduction to the morale boosting Egyptian booklet analyzes the supposed Moslem ideal of killing out the Jews:

> "Regarding the Jewish enemy, Egyptian Chief of Staff Lieutenant General Sa'ad Shazli instructs his men: 'Kill them wherever you find them.' This is an allusion to a verse in the Qur'an (Koran) cited at times in Egyptian indoctrination pamphlets. He warns his troops that the Jews are a treacherous people and may merely feign surrender so as to kill their captors. He orders: 'Kill them, and let not compassion or mercy for them seize you.' "

The booklet urged the Egyptian soldiers into battle with some rather fantastic "history" of past Islamic conquests:

"The Arabs, before Islam, had extensive experience of war and did not fear death. But they did not accomplish then what they did after Islam, when they conquered, in less than one hundred years, an area that extended from Siberia in the north to the Indian Ocean in the south, and from China in the east to the heart of France in the west."

No wonder the Egyptian soldier resented Israel in 1973! If one believed that the religion of Islam had conquered the entire eastern hemisphere, what right had the Jews to this portion of it? It is amazing that such a paragraph could be foisted on twentieth-century people, regardless of their level of education. It should be appreciated that one million copies of the book were published!

The booklet text dealt with the tendency of the Egyptian army to take to headlong retreat under fire, with scripture from the Koran:

"O believers, when you encounter the unbelievers marching to battle, turn not your backs to them. Whoso turns his back that day to them, unless withdrawing to fight again or removing to

join another host, he is laden with the
burden of God's anger, and his refuge is
Gehenna—an evil homecoming! (Koran
8.15, 16).''

The following quotation is a masterpiece of
quoting scripture out of context (Koran scripture).
Note how very little the snippets of scripture,
woven within the paragraph, have to do with the
logic of the entire lesson:

''The Islamic Academy has chosen for
the soldier the absolutely supreme war
ideology; namely, the Holy War for the
sake of Allah. Allah has made the Holy
War the sublime duty by which he en-
nobled the Islamic nation, as is understood by His saying: ' . . . and struggle
for God as is His due, for He has chosen
you . . .' (Koran 22.78) . . . . The objec-
tive of the Holy War, then, is to elevate
the Word of Allah and maintain the
glory of the nation of Muhammad. This
action is indicated in His saying: ' . . .
yet glory belongs unto God, and unto
His Messenger and the believers . . .'
(Koran 63.8).''

Holy writ somehow becomes the foundation of holy war, though the careful reader of the Koran could never excuse the misconstructions above.

The booklet reaches the grand conclusion:

> "Allah's wisdom has decreed that the nation of Muhammad be a nation engaged in the Holy War . . . Allah has inextricably joined faith with the Holy War, so that faith ceases when one flees or shrinks from (it)."

So it becomes sin to retreat or to not kill in the name of Allah.

The Koran is then skillfully quoted against the Jews:

> "Cursed were the unbelievers of the Children of Israel by the tongue of David, and Jesus, Mary's son; that, for their rebelling and their transgression (Koran 5.78)."

Allah is Scripturally accurate in that observation. The unbelievers among the children of Israel, as well as the unbelievers of every other nation (and especially Egypt) were cursed for rebelling and transgression even by God Himself. This hardly makes the Chosen People become the enemies of King David or Jesus, however.

The booklet was dated 29 Jumada I 1393 A.H. (June 30, 1973), in order to have the propaganda ready well before the Yom Kippur attack (some three months before!). The question now is, where are those million booklets? Who might be reading them today?

Obviously, a nation the size of Egypt doesn't distribute many books in one million copies; this one was considered extremely important. More than enough were printed for the army, so that the civilian population was also well equipped. With its deeply anti-Israeli philosophy and its pretense of piety, such a publication must have a profound effect on its readers even today.

The booklet, of course, represents only one facet of typical war propaganda. What of the other anti-Semitism that was rampant just four years ago in the nation of Egypt? The educated elite of Cairo might well keep in step with President Sadat in the new peace offerings, but what of the unlearned tens of millions who are the real population and the real might of Egypt? They were primed in a hate-Israel campaign so recently, and now they are supposed to accomplish an about-face. We might well wonder if the average Egyptian isn't a bit confused by now. We might question whether this nation is really 100% behind its peacemaking leader.

We might well conclude that four wars in quick succession, plus vitriolic propaganda of the kind represented by the shirt-pocket booklet, might have a more profound effect on Egypt than a weekend stint in Jerusalem by its President. The attitude of the Red Sea Pharaoh is probably alive and well in Egypt.

FAIR-WEATHER FRIENDS

So there is opposition to Sadat's peace ideal throughout the Arab world, in Israel to some degree, and undoubtedly in Egypt itself. But that localized opposition doesn't begin to express the animosity of the rest of the world toward peace in the Middle East.

It might be surprising to some for the author to observe that the world doesn't really want peace in the Middle East, but it really seems so apparent. There are three major "worlds" today on planet earth: The Free World; the Communist Bloc; and the so-called Third World. Americans are used to thinking that everybody wants peace everywhere all the time, but there is no real evidence to suggest that any of the three great confederacies is really trying to make it happen.

With the Free World, we hear all sorts of talk about peace, usually led by the American government. Israel is still very popular in the United States, according to recent polls, and Americans have a justifiable respect for the plucky young democracy that has ably flourished and defended itself over the past thirty years. There has been some indication in the press that Sadat's peace conference really was initiated by private correspondence with President Carter. It may fairly be said that the United States would prefer an equitable solution to Middle Eastern problems and real peace for Israel.

But in the rest of the Free World, there is not so much enthusiasm. In the following chapter, we will detail the antagonistic attitudes of Great Britain and France, which nearly caused the annihilation of Israel in 1973. During the oil boycott, only the Dutch opened their harbors and ran the blockade, out of all the nations of the entire Free World. Israel has only fair-weather friends at best throughout Europe, and justifiably calls America her only ally.

As to the Communist bloc, it is to the Russian

way of thinking very advantageous to have continuing unrest in the world. Obviously this expansionist nation favors greater conflict, bloodshed and a steadily divided and weakened Free World. In the following chapter, "The Russians Are Coming," we will detail completely just how obnoxious to the Communist world it would be if there were peace in the Middle East.

As a principle, the Communist philosophy would not applaud the settling of international issues of any sort. They would not, therefore, favor the complete annihilation of Israel and the establishment of a Palestinian state in its place. This would stabilize the Middle East and give the Russians no further excuse to extend their influence and weaponry. They would have to undertake the creation of new animosities, a painstaking process. For their purposes, the Russians prefer an ongoing struggle everywhere. Peaceful relations between nations of the world are counterproductive to Russian motives and often very inconvenient. China, insofar as she is forthrightly Communistic, must necessarily embrace the same world takeover philosophy.

To the Third World, Israel is something of a danger. She is a typical example of "American Imperialism." She "causes" oil boycotts, she harbors Jews, whom nobody likes, and she makes Palestinians commit acts of terrorism. The Third World knows all about oil and guns, and would rather appease those who can provide them than see peace in the Middle East.

The peculiar sort of world "revolutionaries" who hijack airplanes, kidnap government officials and boast of some sort of international network of highly-trained dissidents relate to this Third World attitude of considering Israel imperialistic. Whether the terrorists are in Germany, South America or the Orient, they somehow try to connect themselves to the Palestinian cause, identifying with what they think of as the "freedom fighters" of the Middle East. Color them basically Red.

The Third World and Communist Bloc now have so vast a vote in the United Nations that that supposedly neutral organization has become a rubber stamp for condemning Israel, and implicitly, the United States. Little Israel, with its population of 3,000,000—smaller than so many *cities* of the world—is incessantly censured for this and that, week in and week out. One wonders how that small nation, detested by almost the whole world, as it seems to be, can continue to exist.

Unless one believes in God.

AFTER CAIRO?

The Geneva Conference is supposed to follow the Cairo Conference. The United States and the Soviet Union are the unlikely co-chairmen.

The following chapter is entirely devoted to the Russian deceptions of the future, insofar as Biblical prophecy leads us. It is apparent that the motives of the United States in the upcoming conference at Geneva are not entirely pure, either.

A shrewd letter to the Editor of *Time* magazine brought out an interesting point (December 19, 1977). The reader suggested that there was devilish mischief behind the scenes and that the entire Sadat visit was "hatched with Washington in mind." The plot went this way, in the reader's mind: Washington persuades Sadat to visit Israel and ask Begin to return "all territories held since the 1967 War." And then he would also ask that Israel step aside so that a Palestinian state could be created within its present borders. Washington, of course, would know full well that Israel could not begin to make such concessions at this time. Begin would be forced to offer only token concessions, relative to those asked for. Then Washington would have a new excuse for castigating Israel (not to speak of the rest of the world) and might then be able to get some advantage, perhaps, with Russia or the oil 'producers of the Middle East. It's certainly no secret that Saudi Arabia, the major oil producer and an important controller of the world price of oil, is the real backer of Egypt and Sadat. Could we be seeing a subtle courtship of Saudi Arabia by the United States through this roundabout means? Or possibly some behind-the-scenes deal with Russia? The reader suggested that Washington support Israel and not the Palestinians, in deed as well as in word.

Obviously, the political machinations of the day are beyond the scope of this little book and admittedly, its author. Probably the whole story, with all of its hidden plots, is well beyond the comprehension of even those heads of state directly involved. Middle Eastern politics taxed the considerable brains of such as Joshua, David, the brilliant Solomon and 100 other worthies of ancient times.

WORLD WAR III?

But all the same, it is in *their* writings and the other books of the Bible that we can find a plausible answer. From this point on, the author will refer consistently to the Scriptures in discussing the situation with Russia, the possible appearance of the Antichrist, Armageddon and finally, the establishment of the Kingdom of God on earth.

There will be war, not peace, by and by. The reader is reminded of the Scriptural admonition which describes men proclaiming "peace, peace, when there is no peace." When we have finished all of our peace conferences and made our ultimate peace covenant, we will somehow find ourselves in the greatest war of them all.

Read on!

4

The Russians Are Coming

You've got to hand it to the Russians. Back around the turn of the century, they were a nation of peasants with a few highly cultured intellectuals and total beginners in the industrial revolution.

But now, they can think realistically about taking over the entire world!

That is Communist doctrine—a world takeover—and that is what the Communists have been attempting. A glance at Russian expansion since the Bolshevik Revolution of 1917 will demonstrate in a moment that the Reds are landgrabbers without peer in all of history. In a little over a half century, they have extended their influence over territory that would make Napoleon, all the Caesars, and Alexander the Great bow in real admiration. If their expansion were to continue at the present rate, the world would be speaking Russian in less than a century—or else!

The Communists have cruised over sovereign nations like a bowling ball knocking down so many pins. All of Eastern Europe, with its colorful and diverse cultures, has fallen under the Communist yoke. Almost all of Asia is Red now, as well. Several Middle Eastern and African nations have also fallen under Communism, or at least are motivated in their politics by the Kremlin. The so-called Domino Theory, advanced sometime during the Cold War years, has gathered more and more credence. Nations tumble down like so many dominoes as the Russians advance.

Will Russia actually take over the world? Not really, according to Biblical prophecy. Actually, they will take on one nation too many. They will attack a nation so advanced, so mighty and so resolute that Russia will fall to her knees and be virtually crushed as a world power.

That nation is Israel.

STUBBORN DOMINOES

The dominoes are becoming harder and harder for Russia to knock over these days. The sweep over eastern Europe was infinitely easier than such exercises as South Korea and South Viet Nam. South Korea, of course, remains a free state, such as its freedoms go, but most of Southeast Asia has fallen. However, it cost the Russians many years and many expensive weapons to gain relatively little ground.

And in the Middle East the going has been toughest of all. Russia must think of her Arab allies as among the most tedious of her friends. They eat up time, weapons, financial aid and technological advice as if Russia had 1,000 years to get done with this part of the world. The Arabs cannot seem to pry that handful of Israelis loose from Palestine no matter how much help they get from Moscow, and Moscow must be feeling pretty exasperated by now.

The Middle East would be quite a plum for Russia, of course, with its vast oil fields and its strategic location. The Communists would control the crossroads of the world, cutting off the West from the Far East and dominating the trade routes of virtually all nations. Once gaining a secure foothold in the Middle East and Northern Africa, the Communists could easily eat up the confused tribal nations of the Dark Continent. And then only the few countries of Western Europe would be left as Free World allies in the entire Euro-Asian-African land mass. The sometime democracies of India, Pakistan and so forth would be utterly surrounded and easily crushed, and then Russia could get ready to take on the West.

But all that is a Marxian pipe dream as long as thorny problems like the Middle East stand in the way of the overall plan. And no nation is thornier in the thorny Middle East than Israel. As long as Israel holds her own and remains a sovereign democratic nation, the Russians have something like a ''hole'' in their map. They have made considerable progress already in Africa, but they have had to ''jump over'' Israel to accomplish that.

In a Reader's Digest article, ''Russia's Ruthless Reach Into Africa'' (November, 1977), writer David Reed detailed Russia's African progress:

> ''Moscow has established itself as the patron of the black-liberation movements in white-ruled southern Africa, and is rapidly spreading its influence over a growing number of Marxist-oriented countries elsewhere on the continent. The Russians are supplying arms to keep five separate African wars or guerrilla insurrections going.

> ''Moderate African leaders are increasingly alarmed at what they regard as Africa's newest and most dangerous imperialism. President Felix Houphouet-

Boigny of the Ivory Coast warns: 'Russia will take advantage of any confusion or chaos in Africa to infiltrate the continent. This may go under the guise of aid to so-called liberators but, once inside, the 'benefactors' will be just another occupation force. Leopold Senghor, the poet-president of Senegal, who shares these concerns, adds: 'After Asia, it's Africa's turn to become the bloody continent, the continent of destablization.' ''

The article shows a map of Africa, giving the countries with pro-Soviet governments and those with present Soviet-backed insurgencies. In all, seven nations are in the first category—Ethiopia, Somalia, Mozambique, Angola, People's Republic of the Congo, Benin and Guinea. The Soviet-backed insurgencies are presently occurring in Rhodesia, South Africa and Namibia (Southwest Africa). It would appear from this current map that a good fourth of this continent is either under pro-Soviet government or well on its way to that fate.

But the Russians certainly have to travel a long way to get to their present arena of activity. It would be much more convenient if they could completely control some modern, sovereign nation closer by—say Israel or Egypt. Or, better yet, Israel *and* Egypt.

A careful comparison of prophecy with current events shows that the Russians may be thinking just that way right now.

THE COMING RUSSIAN INVASION OF ISRAEL

Ezekiel said it over 2,500 years ago, but it certainly bears repeating now.

There is to be a vast invasion of Israel, led by a nation to Israel's "uttermost north." That nation is Russia and the time would appear to be, from all indications in both the Bible and current events, in the very near future.

The author does not intend to prophesy, of course, but does rely on the prophet Ezekiel, who foresaw all of this. In his book with Dr. Thomas S. McCall, *The Coming Russian Invasion of Israel*, (Moody Press, 1974) the authors speculated as follows concerning the invasion:

> "Curiously, Egypt is not mentioned among the antagonists. Will something happen to Israel's perennial enemy before the conflict?"

It is largely the above speculation of four years ago that makes this chapter relevant in this present book. Is a peace covenant with Israel the thing that will have happened to Egypt by the time of the Russian invasion? Is Egypt not listed by Ezekiel among the allies of Russia for the very reason we are currently seeing? Is Egypt perhaps going to be a planned victim of the invasion rather than one of the invaders, as things work out? Is the decline of Russian-Egyptian relations, not at all apparent as recently as 1974, going to be the factor that removes Egypt as an ally? Is Sadat now making peace with the wrong people?

(Actually, friends of Israel are friends of God, if the Bible is to be believed. And if Egypt is targeted by Russia, Russia will be the worse off for it. If Egypt actually makes peace with Israel now, it will be the most important move that country will ever make.)

We should briefly review Ezekiel's predictions about the coming invasion to put everything in its proper place. Ezekiel 38 and 39 give the details of the invasion and the outcome; chapter 37 contains the famous "vision of the dry bones," which clearly establishes the restoration to the Promised Land of the Chosen People in the latter days. Lest we misunderstand Ezekiel, God Himself analyzes that arcane vision:

> "Then He said unto me, Son of man, these bones are the whole house of Israel: behold, they say, Our bones are dried, and our hope is lost: we are cut off from our parts.
>
> Therefore prophesy and say unto them, Thus saith the Lord God; Behold, O my people, I will open your graves, and cause you to come up out of your graves, and bring you into the land of Israel.
>
> And ye shall know that I am the Lord, when I have opened your graves, O my people, and brought you up out of your graves,
>
> And shall put my spirit in you, and ye shall live, and I shall place you in your own land: then shall ye know that I the Lord have spoken it, and performed it, saith the Lord" (Ezekiel 37:11-14).

Other hints throughout the ensuing chapters (" . . . the land that is brought back from the

sword, and is gathered out of many people;''
'' . . . the people that are gathered out of the
nations''—Ezekiel 38:8, 12) firmly establish that
Ezekiel was speaking of modern Israel here.
Ezekiel places this entire section ''in the latter
days'' (38:16), and it is clear that the prophet
must refer to Israel as established after 1948 A.D.

This invasion is sometimes referred to as the
''Gog and Magog'' invasion, because those are the
names applied to the invaders in the Scriptures.
These names, along with several names of the
allies in the invasion, appear in Genesis 10:2-4.
God identifies the nations by how they were
originally established after the Flood, which seems
sensible. After all, if you are going to write a Bible
that will be good for thousands of years, you'd
better get together one set of names and stick to
them.

The Scofield Reference Bible, *The Late, Great
Planet Earth*, and any number of other trusted
reference sources trace the term ''Magog'' to
Russia, which, of course, lies to the uttermost
north of Israel. (On a world globe, as a matter of
fact, a straight line drawn north from Jerusalem
will *pass through* Moscow.) The references to the
cities ''Meshech'' and ''Tubal'' (38:2) has been
identified as relating to Moscow and Tobolsk, a

most clear Biblical identification with the modern names.

People throughout history named their cities and their nations for their important leaders and founders, as we still do. Unquestionable genealogical studies have not only placed Russia and her allies in this invasion, but have come up with a most logical encirclement of Israel. Persia, Ethiopia and Libya. Israel will apparently be hit from all directions except the Mediterranean Sea.

And now we see the impact of the absence of Egypt. Up until Sadat's visit, we would have expected Egypt to be Russia's most eager volunteer. But now, a new scenario can be cautiously drawn. Let us speculate that some kind of peace can be made between Egypt and Israel at this time, and that it holds on for awhile. This will provide Russia her excuse to attack both of them. Hatred of Israel is quite commonplace, so that Russia could just be one of a crowd on that. But a reasonable excuse is needed to hate a former ally. Sadat may have begun to provide it.

We also speculated, in *The Coming Russian Invasion of Israel*, "Will Egypt decrease as a major power among the Arabs by the time of the invasion?" (page 36). With Egypt presently on the outs with the other Arabs and with Russia (and Sadat has made very clear that he has heard more than enough criticism from Moscow), her warmaking power has truly diminished. In 1973, with Russian weapons and Arab allies, Egypt was fearsome and the Israelis, though victorious, were deeply impressed. But, obviously, times have changed. It was Russian power and even Russian personnel that operated the 1973 Sinai Campaign. In the Russian invasion of Israel, those Russian weapons and personnel may be on the other side, turned *against* Egypt.

And then, too, with Sadat making overtures for peace with Israel, the other Arab nations, as we have seen, are at least at present considering Egypt the "bad brother." Egypt has certainly decreased as a major power among the Arabs; at least for the moment.

THE BEGINNING OF THE END

The writer is not trying to establish the cogency of his former speculations, but rather to urge upon the reader the pinpoint forecasts of Ezekiel. Considering the whole panorama since Ezekiel prophesied to a captive people of Judah in Babylon (c. 550 B.C.) up to the present day, it's rather amazing how this prophecy has come into focus. Rather like one of those instant camera photographs, it started out mystical and blurry, and at present our five minute developing time is just about up.

In Ezekiel's time, the prophecy was probably utterly misunderstood. The dispersion the people were suffering at that moment was nothing like that which was to come after Titus and Hadrian finished with the Jews, just following the time of Christ. The restoration of the Jewish people of the world to Israel in 1948 was not comparable to the pitiful handful who resolutely rebuilt their Temple after the Babylonian captivity of that sixth century B.C.

Relations with northern powers in the time of Ezekiel geographically ended at the Caucasus mountains in Turkey, so that the "uttermost north" was simply unknown territory. The rabbis must have puzzled during the A.D. centuries over an invasion of Israel, since, of course, this would do little harm to the dispersed but true owners of the land, the Jewish people. But, in 1948, the prophecy again became something of a reality. Israel was Jewish again, the victim of immediate invasion and, at least for those who could read the handwriting on the wall, a potential Free World member and antagonist of Russia.

But when Israel was first settled, the Russians were among those who recognized the new state diplomatically. Russia may have thought that Israel, with her collective farms—the kibbutzim—seemed socialistic in a way. But the Jewish heritage of freedom for the individual, capitalistic enterprise and respect of God, when all is said and done, would never make for a Communist Bloc nation.

When the time was right for Russia to drop Israel as a friend and instead make alliances with the Arabs, she did that. Communists have no allegiance except to Communism, and Russia couldn't care less who her temporary friends might be at certain junctures in her overall plan. Without going into every detail of Ezekiel 38 and 39, analyzed in many good prophecy books, we might just say that Magog—the Russians—will pick on the wrong people. In one of the most vituperative passages of the Old Testament, Jehovah the Mighty reacts:

> "And it shall come to pass at the same time when Gog shall come against the land of Israel, saith the Lord God, that my fury shall come up in my face.

For in my jealousy and in the fire of my wrath have I spoken, Surely in that day there shall be a great shaking in the land of Israel;

So that the fishes of the sea, and the fowls of the heaven, and the beasts of the field, and all creeping things that creep upon the earth, and all the men that are upon the face of the earth, shall shake at my presence, and the mountains shall be thrown down, and the steep places shall fall, and every wall shall fall to the ground.

And I will call for a sword against him throughout all my mountains, saith the Lord God: every man's sword shall be against his brother.

And I will plead against him with pestilence and with blood; and I will rain upon him, and upon his bands, and upon the many people that are with him, an overflowing rain, and great hailstones, fire, and brimstone.

Thus will I magnify myself, and sanctify myself; and I will be known in the eyes of many nations, and they shall know that I am the Lord" (Ezekiel 38:18-23).

Ezekiel's 39th chapter gives the gory details of the aftermath of the invasion, and they are gory indeed:

"Thou shalt fall upon the mountains of Israel, thou, and all thy bands, and the people that is with thee: I will give thee unto the ravenous birds of every sort, and to the beasts of the field to be devoured" (Ezekiel 39:4).

"And it shall come to pass in that day, that I will give unto Gog a place there of graves in Israel, the valley of the passengers on the east of the sea: and it shall stop the noses of the passengers: and there shall they bury Gog and all his multitude: and they shall call it The Valley of Hamongog.

And seven months shall the house of Israel be burying of them, that they may cleanse the land" (Ezekiel 39:11-12).

LOOK OUT!

An interesting after-effect of the invasion is that

the Israelis will burn the weapons left on the fields
for a certain familiar period of time:

> "And that that dwell in the cities of
> Israel shall go forth, and shall set on fire
> and burn the weapons, both the shields
> and the bucklers, the bows and the
> arrows, and the handstaves, and the
> spears, and they shall burn them with
> fire seven years" (Ezekiel 39:9).

This period of seven years has caused some
analysts to place the Russian invasion at the outset
of the seven-year Tribulation Period. The author
concurs with this view. If the Russian invasion were
part of Armageddon, as other annotators hold,
then the burning of these weapons would go on
for seven years during the Kingdom age on the
earth. This seems a very unlikely situation,
considering the presence of the Lord in Israel and
the entirely changed nature of the population and
social circumstances of the earth.

It is important just where in the Tribulation
Period the Russian invasion is placed. If it were
synonymous with Armageddon, then there would
be plenty of advance warning. We would see the
Antichrist come forth, blaspheming in the

Jerusalem Temple (as explained in the next chapter), and those on earth would have literally years to foresee the invasion. But placing it at the beginning of the Tribulation Period means that it will happen without warning. Those who hold this view expect the Russians to invade Israel as soon as all parts of the puzzle, as supplied by Ezekiel, are in their places.

Sadat's peace offer may just be one of those little angular pieces of a puzzle that seems so hard to work in. Once in its proper place, however, it fits so perfectly.

We could put it this way: If the Russians invade Israel before you finish reading this book, it should surprise no student of the Bible.

THE DAY OF ATONEMENT

We mentioned to some degree above the progress of the animosity of Russia toward Israel since 1948; it saw its ultimate fulfillment to date in the 1973 war, the so-called "Yom Kippur War." In that cowardly attack on a nation fasting and in prayer, Russia took a greater part than many people realize. The Yom Kippur War was, in its way, a preview of the coming Russian invasion of Israel.

The excellent investigative book, *Israel: A Secret Documentary* (Tyndale House, 1975), contained previously unpublished information about that war, and particularly about Russia's part in it. The author, Lance Lambert, was caught by the war in Jerusalem, and he remained to do some inquisitive research. He turned up some fascinating details, which seem remarkable in the light of the present peace talks. It was truly supposed to be a fight to the finish, and Russia should be given full credit for all damages done to Israel.

Lambert writes:

"It was at this point in the war that I first learned of the massive Soviet airlift of arms to Syria and Egypt, which had begun on the first day of the war. Large numbers of Antonov transport planes carrying weapons and replacements began arriving just two hours after the war started. One was landing every three minutes. At the same time that the war began, Russian ships arrived at Latakia, Syria, and Alexandria, Egypt, carrying heavy military replacements for everything that was going to be lost in the war. Three days before the war began the Soviet Union launched two orbital Sputniks, which crossed Israel at the best time for aerial photography. Russia then relayed information to Syria and Egypt as to whether Israel was prepared. This is why the war was originally planned for six o'clock in the evening of Yom Kippur, but was moved up to two o'clock. The Russians had passed on the information that preparations had begun on the Israeli side.

The American airlift did not begin until the tenth day of the war.''

Israel certainly lacked confidence and had to believe in miracles. Lambert quotes Shimon Peres, Minister of Defense:

''The miracle is that we ever win. The Arab nations occupy eight percent of the surface of the world. They possess half the known oil resources and are immensely rich. They have more men in their armies than we have people in our state, and on top of the Arabs come the

Russians, who have built for them a great war machine. On our side we have only America.''

America did help, of course, but some of her allies fell far short of opposing this Russian operation. Concerning the remarkable American airlift, Lambert writes:

''The delay was almost completely caused by the refusal of America's so-called allies, particularly Britain, to grant facilities to the United States for refueling her planes. Britain was so bitter about the airlift that she persuaded her NATO allies to fight it. Germany refused to allow the United States to take weapons from her bases on German soil and put them on Israeli ships in Bremen and Hamburg. Finally Portugal opened up the Azores to United States transport planes, and Israel was saved. Planes then came in almost nose to tail. There was no time to lose. If they had not come, Israel would have been totally lost.''

The British and French placed a so-called ''embargo on arms'' to the Middle East war, but

Arab nonbelligerent countries were able to shift their British and French weapons to the combatants. The British refused spare parts for Israel, even though they had already been paid for, and "the French embargo on Israel, moreover, was so bitter that she would not even allow blood donated by French volunteers to be sent to the Israeli wounded."

We should see one other feature of the 1973 war that suggested the upcoming allied invasion of Israel. Weak nations, who could not conceivably take on Israel themselves, or even in combination, quickly jumped into the war when it appeared the Arabs would win:

> "Many nations joined Egypt and Syria. In the first twelve days Saudi Arabia, Kuwait, Yemen, Iran, Sudan, Libya, Morocco, Algeria, Tunis, and Jordan all joined in on the Arab side. North Viet Nam sent a contingent of pilots to Syria. In the first two weeks of the war, twenty-seven African states broke off relations with Israel. Many of them were the recipients of Israeli aid. Thirty-four states in all, including India, broke off relations in this way. Other countries, which were

supposed to be impartial, were in fact bitterly hostile to Israel—for example, Malta.

The growing isolation of Israel can be seen in all this. People sometimes wonder how Armageddon could ever take place. This war proved that within a few days contingents from all the armies of the world could be in Israel.''

Would those of the Christian faith jump to Israel's aid in a future invasion? That seems awfully doubtful from Lambert's findings:

''Furthermore, with the exception of the moderator of the Church of Scotland, no church leaders condemned the fact that the war was a premeditated attack on the most sacred day in the Jewish calendar. The Israeli Cabinet felt very bitter about this. Some of them said, 'We never expected Christian churches to support us in the war, nor would we ever expect Christian churches to collect money for ammunition or weapons. We did not even expect them to collect money for our wounded. But we thought that the least they could do was to stand up and say that they thought it was a terrible thing that on the most sacred and holy day of the Jewish calendar, when everyone was fasting and praying, this premeditated attack took place.'

The Pope just talked about the need for peace on both sides, and said that one could not blame the Arabs for longing for their old homelands. The World Lutheran Federation remained absolutely silent, as did the Anglican Church. The World Council of Churches sent $2 million worth of aid to Jordan, and an undisclosed sum to the Palestinians, which probably means the terrorists. Until that time the World Council of Churches had never sent even one dollar to Israel. However, because of bitter complaints from church bodies within Israel, for the first time in its history it sent five and one-half tons of medical equipment there!

A friend of mine, who is an Anglican clergyman in western England, asked the secretary of the British Council of Churches whether this information were true. He was told, 'I am sorry to say that it is. You must understand that of course there are no Jews represented on the World Council of Churches, so there is no Jewish voice to say anything.' The secretary added, 'We also have a growing left-wing, radical influence in the World Council of Churches, and I am sorry to say that they outvote the rest of us.' He also mentioned that the sum sent to Palestinians exceeded the $2 million sent to Jordan.''

The point is not to indict any particular parties here, but merely to emphasize the fact that world hatred of Israel, a reality of the Tribulation Period, became obvious in 1973 and is even more aggravated today. When it comes to the proper boil, Russia will take full advantage. When Russia feels she has enough sympathizers, she'll go to Israel to make the kill.

One is reminded of World War II, when Russia, ostensibly attacking Nazi Germany, simply claimed all the territory her armies had passed through in Eastern Europe, and so has kept it under her rule until the present time. The world hated Hitler, and so Russia came to the rescue. It worked before, and the Russians think it will work again.

They just haven't understood yet why Israel wins all these wars.

THY KINGDOM COME!

After his rather frightening chapters on the Russian invasion of Israel, Ezekiel goes immediately and happily into the times of the Kingdom of God on earth. The remainder of his book, chapters 40-48, deal with the explicit instructions on the building of the Millennial Temple, the ruling House of the King. It is most refreshing, when reading Ezekiel, to pass from that ferocious invasion into the glory that is to be ours in the coming age.

And so this book will also end with an explanation of the Kingdom to come. Unfortunately, however, there will be a few painful details, if we understand Biblical prophecy correctly, between the Russian invasion of Israel and the return of Jesus Christ. We will have to introduce a character now who has recently become very popular in books, movies and occult worship.

As if the Russians weren't enough, Israel will have to confront the Antichrist!

5

Enter the Antichrist?

Is Sadat the Antichrist?
Or Begin? Or Arafat?
Or O. J. Simpson? Or Woody Allen?

The author does not intend to be facetious, but the point should be made that guessing at the identity of the Antichrist is a losing game. It's been going on virtually since the time of the epistles to the first-century churches, which pointed out advisedly enough that the "spirit of the Antichrist" was already loose in the world. True enough, according to Biblical revelation, an actual person will emerge as *the* Antichrist, but the *spirit* of the Antichrist has been with us since the cross. It is simply the philosophy that does not believe in Jesus Christ, His sacrifice, His resurrection, His atoning work. It is secularism, materialism, worldliness. It is pride and blasphemy. It is incontinence and selfishness. And it is, particularly, assigning to men the works that are God's.

Most specifically, as we shall see, it is the crediting of mere men as being capable peace-makers. It is the confidence that man is in charge of his own destiny and will bring himself to magnificent heights of perfect peace. It is the distrust, and even the hatred, of the Prince of Peace that identifies the spirit of the Antichrist.

SHOTS IN THE DARK

Most recently, Nelson Rockefeller has been the Antichrist in the fantasy of some who would help God fulfill His prophecies. Before him, Henry Kissinger held the honor.

The author hosts a daily radio talk show on KPBC-AM in Dallas, and entertains a wide variety of sometime Bible readers, as well as humbling experts at the Scripture. Sometimes those whose zeal for finding the Antichrist has gotten the best of their scholarship call in with entire prophecy systems set up around a single personality. At the moment (and, of course, the reader realizes that this is merely an off-the-record report of the opinions of some rather opinionated radio listeners), Rockefeller is being accused because of his connection to the Trilateral Commission. The Trilateral Commission is an involvement of free-world economic powers, including the United States, Western Europe and Japan, apparently in its formative stages. The intention of the Commission, so the publicity goes, is to form an economic alliance that would reliably support those Free World members in a shaky international market dangerously threatened by both the Communist and Third World blocs. This emphasis on economic affairs has suggested to some those characteristics of the Antichrist having to do with his economic domination of the world:

> "And he causeth all, both small and great, rich and poor, free and bond, to receive a mark in their right hand, or in their foreheads:
>
> And that no man might buy or sell, save he that had the mark, or the name of the beast, or the number of his name" (Rev. 13:16-17).

The Antichrist certainly has many other characteristics, which we will review in this chapter, but it seems to be in vogue today to emphasize his economic policies. It might also be relevant to say that Nelson Rockefeller, by simply being wealthy, incurs the wrath of many who are not. Much farfetched political commentary was aimed at Rockefeller when he ascended to the Vice Presidency after the Watergate scandal, and one rather notorious Washington-based government analyst indicated that it was the end of the American government: Rockefeller would surely ascend to the throne and become the first "King of America." The commentator gave an exact date upon which President Ford was to abdicate and declared that there would be no further American elections. Such incredible constructions of political events run on a par with accusations about the identity of the Antichrist, of course.

Henry Kissinger came into popularity as a possible Antichrist simply by being a peacemaker. Indeed, through his remarkable "shuttle diplomacy," he even made a workable peace for Israel; undeniably a characteristic of the Antichrist (Dan. 9:27), as we will explain further on. Kissinger, being Jewish, appealed to those who hold that the Antichrist will be a Jew. And thirdly, the former Secretary of State seemed to be well liked in all government circles—even behind the Iron Curtain. The Antichrist, the Scripture indicates, will be welcomed as something of a hero on a white horse (Rev. 6:2). Apparently, the Antichrist will have a great deal of personal magnetism and will engender the trust of diverse governments in his rise to power.

It should be pointed out that Rockefeller and Kissinger cannot both be the Antichrist, and further that Kissinger has already passed from consideration and Rockefeller is temporarily the front-runner. In simpler terms, someone will always be the Antichrist for those who insist on finding him, and *that* someone will pass quickly in and out of fashion as times change.

Looking further back in our own century, we find what may have seemed to be more reasonable accusations in the cases of Adolph Hitler and Joseph Stalin. Those two, of course, had the total dictatorial power which is the hallmark of the Antichrist. Both ruled with iron fists, both divided peoples (declaring some superior and some inferior—and the Jews most emphatically inferior in both cases), and both were somehow able to guide the destinies of millions.

But again, of course, we have only fractions of the total Biblical picture of the Antichrist. Hitler was far too maniacal; the Antichrist, we gather from Scripture, is something of a diplomat—at least at the beginning of his career. Stalin reigned for an inexorably long time; careful readers of

Scripture should have concluded early on that he survived well beyond the seven-year tenure of the Antichrist and still came nowhere close to world domination.

And so it went, reaching back to World War I and its antiheroes. World War I was characterized by many as Armageddon itself—"the war to end all wars"—and one American cult still believes that it was. Going on further back, Popes have been accused of being the Antichrist, as has Napoleon, the Inquisitors, the Crusaders, the Moslems who placed the Dome of the Rock on the Temple site of Jerusalem, and the Roman emperors who oppressed the Jews—particularly Hadrian who also desecrated the Temple site (135 A.D.).

And so, in view of all the accusations that have been made in the past and of the constant presence of those who seek out this colossal villain of world affairs, is it now going to become the turn of Anwar Sadat? Is the smiling, ingenious President of Egypt now to rise to power in the imaginations of those who have switched devils along with the times?

Hopefully not. President Sadat has a long way to go before he fulfills all of the characteristics of the Antichrist as given in the Scriptures. It might

be well for us to review the Biblical highlights of
this extraordinary personality who will represent
the denouement of God's plan and the combined
effects of virtually all of the sin since the Garden of
Eden.

THE BIBLICAL ANTICHRIST

The Antichrist of the Bible is simply an
incomparable character. That is what makes it so
difficult to identify him before his actual
Scripturally-announced characteristics come forth.

He is much more of a peacemaker than any
ordinary mortal we've seen proposing peace plans.
He is much more of a blasphemer than the garden
variety secularists and atheists that haunt the world
scene today. He is much more of a false messiah
than those cultists promising instant salvation to
those flocks of well-scrubbed youngsters of the
stadiums and airports. And he is infinitely greater
a conqueror than those fearsome dictators of our
century and all of their forebears in the history of
earthly warfare.

He is virtually a supernatural being, demon-
strating seemingly supernatural powers, and he
seems to go out of his way to counterfeit Jesus
Christ, the only other supernatural being mortal

men have seen on earth. Indeed, our Lord Himself lamented the success to be enjoyed by the Antichrist in gathering disciples and followers:

> "I am come in my Father's name, and ye receive me not: if another shall come in his own name, him ye will receive" (John 5:43).

The key characteristic of the Antichrist is his Middle Eastern peace plan. The Prophet Daniel tells us, "He shall confirm the covenant with many for one week" (9:27), which in Daniel's parlance denotes seven years. The figure of seven years for the Antichrist's career is also borne out in the Book of Revelation as the time of the period usually called the Tribulation Period. Jesus Himself refers to the second half of this period as the "great tribulation such as was not since the beginning of the world to this time, no, nor ever shall be." Revelation 11:1-3 breaks this Great Tribulation down into months and then days for the careful student of prophecy (a Hebrew year equals 360 days in prophecy).

The Antichrist's entire career, then, lasts but seven years—until the second coming of the Lord and the start of the Kingdom, for which we pray,

"Thy Kingdom come, Thy will be done, on earth as it is in heaven." The Antichrist will come on the scene with his "seven year plan" for the Middle East and will exit via Armageddon.

It appears in Scripture that the Antichrist is European, or at least from out of the territory identified today as Europe. The Prophet Daniel, to whom we owe much of our knowledge of our own future, indicated the Antichrist's kingdom as the fourth world dominating kingdom, or Rome, in Daniel's reckoning (Daniel 7:23-24). The Book of Revelation concurs in a very specific way, describing the Antichrist as a ten-headed beast (Rev. 13:1). The ten heads are taken by prophecy analysts to represent the last alliance of governments occupying the European and Mediterranean area as a kind of revived Roman Empire. Daniel is quite clear:

> "And the ten horns out of this kingdom
> are ten kings that shall arise . . ." (Dan.
> 7:24).

Hal Lindsey's definitive prophecy book, *The Late, Great Planet Earth*, published some eight years ago, identified the Antichrist's territory in this unmistakable way: "We believe that the

Common Market and the trend toward unification of Europe may well be the beginning of the ten-nation confederacy predicted by Daniel and the Book of Revelation.''[1]

Lindsey's theory has received much corroboration in recent years with the extension of the Common Market and its headquarters in Rome, the Club of Rome with its economic forecasts and pronouncements, and even the Trilateral Commission which some think will have Europe as its base.

It might also be said that there is an intimation in Scripture that the Antichrist himself will originate out of the Middle East. One of Daniel's stunning prophetic visions concerning the Greco-Syrian powers describes a future ''king of fierce countenance.'' Daniel seems to characterize the Antichrist with clarity and with much corroboration from other Scripture:

> ''And in the latter time of their kingdom, when the transgressors are come to the full, a king of fierce countenance, and understanding dark sentences, shall stand up.
>
> And his power shall be mighty, but not by his own power: and he shall destroy wonderfully, and shall prosper, and prac-

tise, and shall destroy the mighty and the holy people.

And through his policy also he shall cause craft to prosper in his hand; and he shall magnify himself in his heart, and by peace shall destroy many: he shall also stand up against the Prince of princes; but he shall be broken without hand" (Dan. 8:23-25).

Conceivably then, the Antichrist will have a Middle Eastern origin, but will rise to power on the European political scene.

And so, for those who wish to make Sadat the Antichrist, or Begin, or Arafat, or any other of the Middle Eastern leaders, such a thing is remotely possible. It should be said, however, that working out complex prophecies can be a highly speculative exercise in itself, and readers are urged to consult the Scriptures and the prophetic books that have stood the test of time in seeking this knowledge. There are those, of course, to whom Biblical prophecy means nothing, and they and their ancestors have been, and will always be, surprised by events that precisely follow the announced course of God's will.

One of the Antichrist's apparently supernatural works is his recovery from what appears to be a mortal wound (Rev. 13:13-14). He is "resurrected" from this fatal blow rather in the manner of the true Christ, whom he consistently copies. The insinuations of the PLO and other Arab powers that the Egyptian army would do well to deal with Sadat (read "assassinate") might set up such a resurrection in the minds of those who wish to see Sadat as the supernatural Antichrist.

It is not the Antichrist's magic, of course, but Satan's. The Scripture is very clear:

> "And they worshipped the dragon which gave power unto the beast . . ." (Rev. 13:4).

BAD WILL TOWARD MEN

As a personality, the Antichrist is a supreme egotist, and a blasphemer without equal in all of man's long history of blasphemy. Hitler-like, he establishes a personality cult based on adoration of himself. Virtually the whole world will fall into the trap (Rev. 13:8), and will worship their new leader with a fanaticism not seen since Nazi Germany.

He will have a front-man called the "False

Prophet'' (Rev. 16:13). This False Prophet, variously identified today as Rev. Moon, Jeanne Dixon, President Carter, and so many other public figures who have something to do with either prophecy or world affairs, will do public relations for the Antichrist. He will create a lifelike replica of the world leader, capable of speech, according to the Scriptures. Inevitably, Sadat has also been accused of being the False Prophet, as has Rockefeller, Kissinger, et. al.

His peace plan for the Middle East will work at first. Apparently, his military power and expedient political relationships will be enough to guarantee the peace for a time. However, as the astute Daniel observed, the Antichrist ''by peace shall destroy many'' (Dan. 8:25). His economic system will apparently create one worldwide currency, or perhaps the elimination of currency. Rev. 13:16-18 indicates that every citizen will bear a mark on his right hand and forehead, and without it the individual would not be permitted to buy or sell anything. The number 666 is given cryptically in the Scripture as the number of the beast.

We shall not go into the endless corridors of numerology searching for the meaning of 666, which has been done adequately, or rather inadequately, by prophecy hobbyists the world around. Suffice it to say that the number remains a mystery, although some fascinating theories have been advanced. The idea of people buying and selling by number, however, has enormous credence when one considers that the Book of Revelation was certainly written well before such a thing was imaginable. The credit card buying of today dovetails so perfectly with this Biblical passage that by itself it makes Revelation appear to be written very recently.

It is certainly conceivable at this time, with computer technology being what it is, that a worldwide buying and selling system could be in the offing. After all, cash is cumbersome, tempting to thieves and hopelessly polyglot. As the world becomes a smaller place and nations deal with dozens of other nations, a simpler form of exchange must eventually be necessary.

Something like the Antichrist's solution is already in progress, with experimental markings on grocery products read by special machines at the cashier's counter. It would be just another small step to having the customer carry a card identifying his bank account, which the computer could charge. And, finally, with the inevitable theft and loss of cards, the number could be placed indelibly on the individual's skin. One is reminded of the invisible stamps, placed usually on the back of the hand, at amusement parks or dances when an individual wishes to leave and return. Under a special light, the mark is visible and the individual identified. Why on the hand and the head? Well, the hand is already being used and is easy to extend toward a machine. But should this system become worldwide practice, it will be found more convenient, since some have lost limbs and others temporarily must wear casts and slings, to place the mark where it can never be lost—on the forehead. Presumably, no one without a head will be buying or selling anything.

THE MAN WHO WOULD BE GOD

The Antichrist's ultimate blasphemy and clearest identification feature will be his stupefying actions in connection with the rebuilt Temple of God in Jerusalem. This Tribulation Temple will become a target of the ever more powerful Antichrist, and in the midst of the Tribulation Period he will enter the Temple and declare that he is God!:

"Let no man deceive by any means: for that day shall not come, except there come a falling away first, and that man of sin be revealed, the son of perdition;

Who opposeth and exalteth himself above all that is called God, or that is worshipped; so that he as God sitteth in the Temple of God, shewing himself that he is God" (II Thess. 2:3-4).

This singular character will not mean that he is *equal* to God or that he is *to be regarded* as God; he *is* God, he will declare!

Thus desecrating the holiest shrine of the very people with whom he initially made a peace covenant, the Antichrist will bring on Armageddon. That great war, involving the armies of virtually the entire globe, will take some three and one-half years to merely mobilize.

Revelation 16:13-16 chronicles the massive might of the Antichrist's armies gathered together in that quiet, beautiful, level valley called Armageddon. It lies in the northern part of Israel, extending from the Mediterranean some 40 miles eastward to the Sea of Galilee.

The battle of Armageddon also marks the second coming of the Lord (Rev. 19:11-14), and the Antichrist then meets his doom. The man who would be God, along with his False Prophet, is no more:

> "These both were cast alive into a lake of fire burning with brimstone" (Rev. 19:20).

GETTING IT ALL TOGETHER

Hopefully, the above analysis from Scripture, briefly stated as it must be in this space, will show that there is much more to identifying the Antichrist than picking out some likely or unpopular public figure. Anwar Sadat, or anyone else alive at the moment, for that matter, does not begin to fulfill even the few characteristics given above.

Interestingly, however, many personalities throughout recent history have exhibited *certain* qualities of the Antichrist, and it seems to be just a matter of time until someone comes along who will get it all together. The Antichrist's personality cult is certainly suggestive of the mindless worship of Hitler that permeated a nation of otherwise civilized people. Henry Kissinger's peacemaking on behalf of Israel is most suggestive of the Antichrist's more comprehensive peace covenant. The economic concerns of Rockefeller, legitimate as they are on today's world scene, certainly portend a like international problem-and-solution situation the Antichrist must face. Certainly, President Sadat has proved so far to have a likeable personality and an apparently commendable attitude toward peace in the Middle East, and the normal economic concerns of a national leader today. Perhaps he even has a certain diplomatic charm; though nothing to equal the Antichrist's veritably hypnotic personality.

In conclusion, we can only say that President Anwar Sadat's peace gesture follows a trend. Truly, it is justifiable to point out that all of those who step forward with an idea for peace in the Middle East help set up the Antichrist's ultimate covenant.

Sadat's move was more dramatic than Kissinger's, and his solutions, at least as announced, seem more comprehensive, at this writing. It might be fair to say that we have moved somewhat closer to the time of the Antichrist in this particular area, but we could not say more than that.

Quite probably, no one we know is the Antichrist.

But just as probably, he is alive today, somewhere among us.

1. Hal Lindsey and C. C. Carlson, *The Late, Great Planet Earth* (Grand Rapids: Zondervan, 1970), p. 94.

6

Visit Israel and See the Pyramids

When all the peace proposals and all the wars have come and gone, Israel and Egypt will be friends. In the Kingdom to come, these two perennial combatants will be like one nation, and even Syria, so hostile to Israel at the moment, will be part of the friendship.

Today, if one wishes to visit both Israel and Egypt, or Israel and Syria, there is a serious passport problem. As matters now stand, one is required to go to a neutral point first when passing across these unfriendly borders. But in the great age of peace to come, the antagonists of the Middle East will be true brothers in peace. The tourists will have no problems at the borders, for as God Himself exalts:

"In that day there shall be a highway out
of Egypt (through Israel) to Assyria, and
the Assyrian shall come into Egypt, and

the Egyptian into Assyria, and the Egyptians shall serve with the Assyrians" (Isaiah 19:23).

ISAIAH SPEAKS

There are broad sections of prophecy concerning Egypt in the Old Testament, but they are all consummated in the magnificent and beautiful chapter, Isaiah 19. Jeremiah 46, Zechariah 14, and the lengthy analysis of Ezekiel, chapters 29-32, give a great many details about Egypt in prophecy. But Isaiah's beneficent remarks tie all the predictions together in one of the truly satisfying prophecies of peace.

Isaiah's chapter is not easy to understand, but Wilbur Smith, whom we credited earlier, and other theologians, have analyzed it very completely. "The Burden of Egypt," as the chapter is "titled," reviews in 25 verses the thousands of years of Egypt's important Biblical career.

The first sixteen verses of the chapter are devoted to judgments on Egypt by God, which have been fulfilled through the ages. God predicted the idolatry of Egypt:

"And the spirit of Egypt shall fail in the midst thereof; and I will destroy the counsel thereof: and they shall seek to the idols, and to the charmers, and to them that have familiar spirits, and to the wizards" (Isaiah 19:3).

God was not impressed with the worldly wisdom of the Egyptians:

"Surely the princes of Zoan are fools, the counsel of the wise counsellors of Pharaoh is become brutish: how say ye unto Pharaoh, I am the son of the wise, the son of ancient kings?

Where are they? Where are thy wise men? And let them tell thee now, and let them know what the Lord of hosts hath purposed upon Egypt" (Isaiah 19:11-12).

And God was not impressed with the strength of Egypt, predicting that the Israelis would overcome it:

"In that day shall Egypt be like unto women: and it shall be afraid and fear because of the shaking of the hand of the Lord of hosts, which He shaketh over it.

And the land of Judah shall be a terror unto Egypt, every one that maketh mention thereof shall be afraid in himself, because of the counsel of the Lord of hosts, which he hath determined against it" (Isaiah 19:16-17).

But when all these judgments and troubles are over with, there follows some of the most hopeful and serene promises in all of prophecy. We should appreciate these thoughts in their full context:

"And the Lord shall be known to Egypt, and the Egyptians shall know the Lord in that day, and shall do sacrifice and oblation; yea, they shall vow a vow unto the Lord, and perform it.

And the Lord shall smite Egypt: he shall smite and heal it: and they shall return even to the Lord, and he shall be intreated of them, and shall heal them.

In that day shall there be a highway out of Egypt to Assyria, and the Assyrian shall come into Egypt and the Egyptian into Assyria, and the Egyptians shall serve with the Assyrians.

In that day shall Israel be the third with Egypt and with Assyria, even a blessing in the midst of the land:

Whom the Lord of hosts shall bless, saying, Blessed be Egypt my people, and Assyria the work of my hands, and Israel mine inheritance'' (Isaiah 19:21-25).

What a glorious future Egypt has, and what a remarkable time of peace in the Middle East!

"AND JEHOVAH SHALL BE KNOWN TO EGYPT"

In the distant past, Egypt knew Jehovah and they learned to fear Him. Going all the way back to Abraham, it is obvious that Pharaoh appreciated the God of heaven and His immense powers.

Joseph frankly told Pharaoh that his own skill at dream interpretation was entirely dependent on the God of Israel. Moses threatened his Pharaoh with plagues from the Almighty, and He delivered in no uncertain terms. That Pharaoh, staggered by the ten brutal plagues and the loss of his entire army in pursuit of the Exodus, cannot have said that he didn't know Jehovah. He may not have liked Jehovah, but he very well knew Him.

But, of course, knowing the Lord and worshipping Him are two different things. Egypt continued in a dark age of paganism, unrelieved even today. It is remarkable to think that the land of the sun god of the age of pyramids, which then progressed through ages of wizards and magicians, various pagan deities, and thirteen centuries of the Islam faith, will someday return to the true God. But the breathtakingly accurate forecasts of Isaiah (such as the invasion of Israel by Babylon, the coming of the Messiah, the restoration of the Jews to Israel in the latter days) must always be taken seriously.

Now, of course, all the nations in the Kingdom will worship the Lord with no exceptions. As Zechariah prophesied:

> "And the Lord shall be king over all the earth: in that day shall there be one Lord, and His name one" (Zech. 14:9).

But Egypt is particularly singled out as a nation that will be, indeed *must* be, faithful to the King of Jerusalem. Zechariah goes on:

> "And it shall come to pass, that every one that is left of all the nations which came against Jerusalem shall even go up from year to year to worship the King, the Lord of hosts, and to keep the feast of tabernacles.
>
> And it shall be, that whoso will not come up of all the families of the earth unto Jerusalem to worship the King, the Lord of hosts, even upon them shall be no rain.
>
> And if the family of Egypt go not up, and come not, that have no rain; there shall be the plague, wherewith the Lord will smite the heathen that come not up to keep the feast of tabernacles.
>
> This shall be the punishment of Egypt, and the punishment of all nations that come not up to keep the feast of tabernacles" (Zech. 14:16-19).

It almost seems as though Zechariah, in emphasizing the importance of appropriate worship at Jerusalem for all nations, singles out Egypt for an example. After all, if we today were to predict just which nation would be the most resistant to pilgrimages to the Jewish Temple, we would certainly come up with Israel's most dependable enemy from across the Sinai. So Zechariah is saying, in effect, "All of you have to do this, even *Egypt*." If Egypt has to do this, then certainly every other nation will be expected to, the prophet assures us.

But getting back to Isaiah's broader view (which comments on the whole of the Kingdom and not just its outset), we can see that Egypt will be glad to worship the Lord. "They shall vow a vow unto the Lord and perform it," Isaiah is happy to report. And the Lord will certainly recognize the worship of Egypt; "And He shall be entreated of them and shall heal them."

Further reviewing Isaiah's wonderful verses, we see Syria enter the picture (Assyria, in Isaiah's reckoning, which may take in more of the northern and eastern Middle East than just Syria). Again, the very brutality toward Israel of ancient Assyria will melt away into peaceful alliance and common worship in the Kingdom. It should be appreciated that in Isaiah's time, the Assyrians were regarded as the most vicious of foreign conquerors, a warring people who terrorized all surrounding nations, took massive groups of captives and unfairly mistreated their spoils. It was Assyria which carried off the ten northern tribes of Israel and moved pagan peoples into the land, who were later called "Samaritans." Assyria dictated life and death to the Middle Eastern world in her days of triumph and pillage.

But unquestionably Assyria is to become part of the family of God, along with Israel and Egypt, according to Isaiah. Each of the three nations receives a special title in the prophet's concluding verse of this chapter: Egypt, "My People;" Assyria, "The Work of My Hands;" and Israel, "Mine Inheritance." The titles seem almost equal in this final, special benediction from the Lord, especially when compared to the long ages when Israel was strictly the "Chosen People," and Egypt and Assyria were just so many countless pagans.

The Middle East will still be in the news every day; undoubtedly, in the Kingdom to come. But the news will all be good.

THE PRESIDENT AND THE KING

Is President Sadat, then, with his new peace offer, leading us to the Kingdom of God? After all, at some point there has to be a transfer from animosity to friendship in Egyptian relations toward Israel.

Obviously, it's too early to say and Sadat's real motives are not completely clear at this writing. But as we have shown in connection with the coming Russian invasion of Israel, a peace agreement between Egypt and the Holy Land is somewhat to be expected before the end. Leading up to the Tribulation Period, when the Russians will invade, something unusual must have happened to Egypt because she is not listed as one of Russia's allies.

But, just as clearly, there won't be *unbroken* peace between Egypt and Israel until the Kingdom itself. Armageddon knows of no peace alliances and the Biblical "King of the South" is taken by most analysts to represent Egypt, or Egypt plus some additional territory in her area. The king of the South will attack at Armageddon.

The best and most cautious scenario might suggest that there will be a temporary peace arrangement between Egypt and Israel before the Russian invasion. After the invasion, peace will continue under the Antichrist's arrangement until the blasphemy in the Temple (II Thess. 2:3-4). Then, all Hell will literally break loose as all nations, certainly including Egypt, will converge against Israel.

In the last battle of Egypt and Israel at Armageddon, when Pharaoh-nechoh met King Josiah, the king of the Jews was slain. In the next battle at Armageddon, the King of the Jews will return in glory and put a stop to all war-making activities of unbelieving men.

Thus, Sadat's initiative may mean something at this time; it may help lead us toward the opening Tribulation Period situation. In that sense, the President of Egypt is helping with God's plan.

But in a greater sense, it is truly the beginning of the end.

EVERYONE IS INVITED

We should not leave the subject of the Kingdom of God on earth without stressing that everyone is invited. Whether you are an Egyptian, a Syrian, a Communist, an atheist or whatever, the door to the Kingdom of God is certainly open.

The Kingdom is for believers, and that means,

Biblically, believers in God and in His entire plan for the redemption of man. Those elected to the Kingdom must believe in Jesus Christ, His sacrifice and resurrection, as entirely filling the need of reconciliation of man with God. Christians of every nation will go into the Kingdom, including those of the presently hostile nations mentioned above; and race, color, creed, etc., are no factors. "God is no respector of persons," Paul found, as he exhorted the Gentiles to salvation (Acts 10:34).

In view of the approaching end times, this is a very good time to think over one's relationship with God. We can safely say that salvation is available "for a limited time only," since prophetic events seem to be progressing rapidly toward the Tribulation Period. The author certainly does not mean to date the Tribulation Period, but only to urge upon unbelieving readers the fact that there is a finite end to this age of grace, and that one's faith is surely a matter of life and death.

Many people regard their faith in Christ to be of a temporal kind—that it will improve this life, but that's all there is to it. But actually, Christianity, and that faith alone, promises a significant future. It is not so much for the blessings received in this life that believers walk with the Lord, although those are very meaningful. But the life to come is of such overwhelming hope and promise that the believers do not even fear death.

The Kingdom will be a powerful place indeed. It will be established under Jesus Christ, the Prince of Peace, and true peace will be maintained. It will not be the sort of hesitant, bargaining peace arrangement we are seeing today in the Middle East, or between America and Russia, but rather genuine global peace, strictly enforced under Divine rule.

The Kingdom is a heavenly conception, established on the earth with Jerusalem as its capital. The regathered, restored and converted people of Israel will inherit the Kingdom, as will believers the world around. Righteousness, not sinfulness, will be the norm as the meek inherit the earth. The knowledge of the Lord will be universal. Satan will be removed from the scene (Rev. 20:1-5), and the human race can progress as it was first meant to before the serpent tempted Eve. Bible annotator C. I. Scofield states:

"It is impossible to conceive to what heights of spiritual, intellectual and physical perfection humanity will attain in this, its coming age of righteousness and peace'' (see Isaiah 11:4-9; Psalms 72:1-10).

God's will shall be done on earth as it is in heaven and all of the goodness, humility and productiveness that each of us innately realizes is possible for the family of man will at last be reality.

Whether our present struggles for peace will provide any lasting good for humanity is unclear; whether Armageddon is just around the corner or a century away is equally unclear; whether man on his own initiative will ever learn to live in peace, without fear of his world being blown up in his face at any moment, seems doubtful. But one thing is *very* clear: The faith in God Almighty and in the redemption of Jesus Christ makes it all academic. The magnificent age of the Kingdom is open to all who believe.

It will be reality someday that one can visit Jerusalem and see Jesus Christ. It will be reality that no one on earth need fear his neighbor someday. It will be reality that someday men will visit Israel and, without passport, weapons or explanations, see the pyramids of Egypt.

Believe that this is true, and the truth will set you free.